The Night Henry Ford Met Santa

By Carol Hagen

Illustrated by Matt Faulkner

I would like to thank Heather Hughes for her instinctive timing of this project
and Aimee Jackson and Judy Gitenstein for breathing new life into my story.
What an awesome experience this has been!
—Carol

Sleeping Bear Press™

310 North Main Street, Suite 300
Chelsea, MI 48118
www.sleepingbearpress.com

THOMSON
✹
GALE™

© 2006 Thomson Gale, a part of the Thomson Corporation.
Thomson, Star Logo and Sleeping Bear Press are trademarks
and Gale is a registered trademark used herein under license.

Printed and bound in Canada.

First Edition

10 9 8 7 6 5 4 3 2 1

Library of Congress Cataloging-in-Publication Data

Hagen, Carol.
The night Henry Ford met Santa / written by Carol Hagen;
illustrated by Matt Faulkner.
p. cm.
Summary: Henry Ford, the creator of the Model T automobile, visits
Santa Claus at the North Pole and, as he watches the elves making toys,
he decides to use the same assembly line method to manufacture
his automobile.
ISBN 1-58536-132-1
1. Ford, Henry, 1863-1947—Juvenile fiction. [1. Ford, Henry, 1863-
1947—Fiction. 2. Santa Claus—Fiction. 3. Assembly-line methods
—Fiction. 4. Automobiles—Design and construction—Fiction.]
I. Faulkner, Matt, ill. II. Title.
PZ7.H1234Ni 2006
[E]—dc22
2006004561

To my son Tyler, who has a passion
for the beauty and magic of Christmas.
— Carol

I dedicate this book to the
children of Michigan.
— Matt

It was a snowy evening, three weeks before Christmas 1908 in Detroit, Michigan. Henry Ford was in his workshop, admiring his new Model T Ford. Henry thought it was the most beautiful car he had ever seen. He wished that everyone in town could own one of his cars. But each car cost a lot of money to make and it cost a lot of money to buy. That meant only rich people owned the Model T.

Back at the house, Henry's wife, Clara, was in the kitchen making supper. The smell of chicken and dumplings filled the air. Edsel Ford, who was eight years old, sat at the table, writing a letter. "Dear Santa," he wrote. "I have been a very good boy. This year I would like a train set and some roller skates. I can't think of anything else. Thank you. Edsel Ford."

"Can we leave Santa some cookies and milk, like we did last year?" he asked his mother.

"That would be a nice idea," Clara answered. "We can also leave some carrots for his reindeer. They work very hard pulling all those toys across the sky. Now son, please put on your coat and boots and go out to the shed and tell Papa to come in for supper."

Edsel bundled up and headed for his father's workshop in the shed behind their house. Outside, he could hear the snow crunch under his feet. He could see his breath form puffs of smoke. The moon was big and bright and it made the field look like it was splashed with moonbeams and glitter.

Edsel gazed up at the big yellow moon and imagined what it must feel like to drive a sleigh across the sky, like Santa. This year on Christmas Eve, Edsel hoped to stay awake long enough to catch a glimpse of Santa and his reindeer flying across the night sky.

Edsel opened the door of the shed. "Hello, Papa!" he said as he shook the snow off his boots and brushed some snowflakes from his eyelashes. "Mama has dinner ready."

"Thank you, son," Henry said as he put on his coat and boots.

"Papa, are you going to ask Santa for anything?" Edsel asked as they walked through the deep snow.

"I don't need a present from Santa, but I could use some advice," said Henry. "I need to find a way to make cars cheaper so that ordinary folks won't have to ride around in horses and buggies any more. It would take a miracle to solve this problem," said Henry.

"Christmas is about miracles, Papa!" exclaimed Edsel. "Write Santa a letter and ask him if he knows a better and faster way to make the Model T. Anyone who can make millions of toys and deliver them in one night must have some good ideas."

After all the dinner dishes had been washed, Clara went into the parlor to read the paper and father and son sat back down at the kitchen table. Edsel rewrote his letter. He took out the line that said "I can't think of anything else," and put in, "Please help my dad solve his problem. I know you can do it."

Henry composed a letter to Santa, too. Here's what it said:

Dear Santa,

My son, Edsel, has urged me to write you this letter. He thinks you can help me. What I need Santa, is your advice.

How is it that you are able to make millions of toys so quickly up at the North Pole? Can you help me find a faster way to make more cars for less money?

Recently I built an automobile called a Model T Ford. There are many people who would like to own one of my automobiles, but don't have enough money. If I could make the car more affordable, doctors could get to patients more quickly. Families could drive to church on Sundays and then enjoy a picnic afterward. More farm children could attend schools in town.

The cost of keeping a car is four times less than owning a horse. I just need a way to make the car cost less to make. Thank you for your help.

Your friend and Edsel's dad,
Henry Ford
Detroit, Michigan

The next morning Henry mailed the two letters on his way to his factory in town. Several nights later everyone in the Ford home was fast asleep. A light snow fell over the city. The only sound in the house was the ticktock of the grandfather clock in the parlor.

In the middle of the night, Henry awoke to a noise on the roof. Then he heard a loud thud and a groan coming from the parlor. He got out of bed and went downstairs.

There in the fireplace was Santa!

"Hello," said Santa.

"What are you doing here?" cried Henry. "It's not Christmas!"

"Aren't you Henry Ford?" asked Santa.

"Well, yes I am."

"Didn't you write me a letter saying you needed some help?"

"Yes, I did write you a letter."

"So, I have come to help you with your problem," said Santa.

"Come with me," he said with a twinkle in his eye.

Santa took Henry up the chimney to his sleigh on the roof.

Henry was surprised at how easy it was to get up the chimney.

After a smooth ride, they arrived at the North Pole.

Henry met Mrs. Claus, who was in charge of feeding the elves. Every day Mrs. Claus and her helpers made delicious sandwiches and pies and hot cider for the elves to feast on.

There were hundreds of elves working in Santa's workshop. Santa greeted every elf and knew each one's name. The workshop was very clean, bright, and even bigger than Henry's factory. The elves were busy making sure all the children got the toys on their Christmas lists.

A HAPPY
WORKSHOP
IS A SAFE
WORKSHOP!

Down the hall was a very big, round room. "This is the Rotunda," Santa said. Seated at a long table were dozens of elves making toy trains. Henry noticed something different about the way they were working. Each elf had only one job to do. One elf cut the wood. The elf next to him pounded the nails as he put on the sides of each car. The next elf painted the train car. The next elf put on the wheels, and so on until the last elf put the finished train car into a beautiful Christmas box with the child's name attached. Henry noticed it took no time at all to make the train cars. This gave him an idea.

INSPECTORS INSPECTING

PACKING AND SHIPPING

"That's it! I'll make my cars the same way the elves are making these trains. I'll set up my factory with everyone in a line just like this one. Each worker will do only one task and pass the car along to the next worker. That worker will do one task until it reaches the end and the car is completely assembled. I'll be able to make hundreds of automobiles in half the time! More people will afford to buy my cars because they'll cost less to make."

As they left the Rotunda, Henry saw many boxes, each one containing a train set for a different child. He noticed one box that said: To Edsel, From Santa.

When Santa dropped Henry off at home, the sun was just coming up. The family was still sleeping and Henry decided he would wait until Christmas day to tell them about his visit to the North Pole.

Christmas morning finally arrived. Edsel woke up and leaped out of bed. The freshly fallen snow looked like a white velvet blanket. "IT'S CHRISTMAS!" he cried. He made such a commotion running down the stairs that his parents woke up, too.

As Edsel ran past the kitchen, he saw that the cookies and carrots were gone and the glass of milk was empty. Edsel howled with delight as he headed for the parlor.

There, under the tree, were his new roller skates and a brand new train set! It was exactly what he had asked for, complete with hills, trees, barns, and miniature houses.

Edsel noticed another box near
the train. The card on the gift read:
To Henry, From Santa.
"Look, Papa!" cried Edsel.
"Santa brought you a present, too!"
Henry unwrapped the gift and smiled.
There in the box was a miniature
Model T Ford.

From the Collections of The Henry Ford

A Special Note to Readers

*T*he *Night Henry Ford Met Santa* is fiction, but it is based on things that really happened in Henry Ford's life. Henry Ford lived in Dearborn, Michigan at his Fair Lane mansion until his death in 1947. Several years ago, while enjoying a guided tour of the mansion, I read Henry's words inscribed above the stairwell: "Whatever is desirable and right is never impossible." As I reflected on his words, I realized the magnitude of his many accomplishments. In many ways, this quote became the guiding idea for my story. I wanted to show that children can teach adults to dream, and that miracles can happen when love flows from an innocent heart and becomes the most unlikely source of inspiration.

As I continued my tour, I got a sense that Christmas struck a tender chord with the Ford family. I learned that Henry and Clara had created a "Santa's Workshop" from a small cabin that was located on the grounds. For thirty years Henry and Clara would host countless school children on a magical adventure to Santa's Workshop during Christmas time. Complete with a sleigh ride, jingle bells, toys, and reindeer (cows with antlers strapped to their heads), and of course Santa. Occasionally, if you looked closely, you would find Henry beneath the white beard.

Edsel Ford really did write a letter to Santa when he was eight years old, but he wrote it in 1901, not in 1908. I used one line from Edsel's original letter and crafted other details to match the ideas I wanted to convey in my story.

Henry Ford built his first car, the Quadricycle, in 1896 and the first Model T in September 1908, just before Christmas, the same time as in the story. The car was built at the Piquette Plant, Ford's factory on Piquette Avenue in Detroit, Michigan.

Until 1913 Henry Ford manufactured his cars one at a time. Mechanics and craftsmen would gather at a central workstation and build one car from beginning to end. This was not very practical because it took a long time. It was also very expensive. Each car cost $850, which was a lot of money in those days.

Around 1913 Henry began to use the method of production known as the assembly line at his factory in Highland Park, Michigan. He had visited a meat-packing plant in Chicago and noticed that an overhead trolley would pass the carcass to each butcher, who then carved specific cuts of meat as it passed by. He decided to try the process with his cars—but in reverse.

Using a rope and a chain, the car would move along to the next worker, until it was fully assembled. After Henry introduced the conveyor belt, things moved faster and the price of the car was reduced to $260, which made it much more affordable. By 1927 fifteen million Model T cars had been sold!

Henry Ford did not invent the assembly line, but he was the first person to use the assembly line to make cars. His method is very similar to the way Santa's elves make train sets in my story. Did Henry Ford learn more about the assembly line from Santa Claus on a visit to the North Pole? Well, you'll just have to decide that for yourself!

I did my research for the story at the Benson Ford Research Center at The Henry Ford in Dearborn, Michigan. The museum has Edsel Ford's original letter to Santa and a lot of other interesting things, too. If you ever get a chance, it's a wonderful place to visit. Or, you can visit the museum online at www.thehenryford.org. Henry Ford's estate, Fair Lane, can be found online at www.henryfordestate.org.

Carol Hagen

Carol Hagen began writing at a very young age, but *The Night Henry Ford Met Santa* is her first published work. After spending several years in southern California working in the film and television industry, Carol returned to Michigan where she completed her B.A. at the University of Michigan-Dearborn and her Master of Library and Information Science at Wayne State University. She is currently a teacher/librarian in a middle school and resides in southeastern Michigan with her family.

Matt Faulkner

Matt Faulkner has written and illustrated a number of children's books. His work has won wide praise for its humor, exuberance, and sensitivity. He is also a contributing illustrator to such national periodicals as *The New York Times*, *The Wall Street Journal*, and *Forbes*. He lives in the southeastern corner of Michigan with his son and their three cats. For more information about Matt, you can visit him at: www.mattfaulkner.com.